Exit Point

Laura Langston

orca soundings

ORCA BOOK PUBLISHERS

Library and Archives Canada Cataloguing in Publication

Langston, Laura, 1958-
Exit point / Laura Langston.
(Orca soundings)

ISBN 10: 1-55143-525-x (bound) / ISBN 10: 1-55143-505-5 (pbk.)
ISBN 13: 978-1-55143-525-1 (bound) / ISBN 13: 978-1-55143-505-3 (pbk.)

I. Title. II. Series.
PS8573.A5832E95 2006   JC813'.54   C2006-900407-2

First published in the United States, 2006
Library of Congress Control Number: 2006921007

Summary: Sixteen-year-old Logan is dead, but he realizes
he still has unfinished business.

Mixed Sources
Cert no. SW-COC-001271
© 1996 FSC

FSC

Orca Book Publishers is dedicated to preserving the environment and has printed this book on paper certified by the Forest Stewardship Council.

Orca Book Publishers gratefully acknowledges the support for its publishing programs provided by the following agencies: the Government of Canada through the Canada Book Fund and the Canada Council for the Arts, and the Province of British Columbia through the BC Arts Council and the Book Publishing Tax Credit.

Cover design by Teresa Bubela
Cover photography by Bigshot Media

ORCA BOOK PUBLISHERS
PO BOX 5626, Stn. B
Victoria, BC Canada
V8R 6S4

ORCA BOOK PUBLISHERS
PO BOX 468
Custer, WA USA
98240-0468

www.orcabook.com
Printed and bound in Canada.

13 12 11 10 • 7 6 5 4

For Kory.

"No act of kindness,
however small, is ever wasted."
—Aesop

Chapter One

He says I died at the wrong time.

I'm not sure I'm dead to begin with.

I'm lying on a bed in a round, white room and I can't move. There are people around me, dressed in gray robes. They hold me down. Not with their hands, but with something.

I stare up to where the ceiling is supposed to be. There is no ceiling, only sky. A pale, bleached-out sky vibrating with an eerie glow. Like a planetarium ceiling before the show starts. There are colors around me too. Moving colors. They quiver and ping and make a wind-chime kind of music.

"I'm dreaming, right?"

No one answers out loud. Instead I hear *his* voice in my head and this is what he says: *There are five exit points in any one life. Five points when a person can die and not mess with the Big Plan.*

"You should have waited for exit point five." Now he speaks into my ear. His breath is hot on my skin. "Instead you took an easier option. You took exit point two."

If I had waited, I would have died on June 9, 2066, at the age of seventy-seven, by choking on a grape.

Instead I died October 28, 2004, in a car that crashed and exploded on Houser Way.

I was sixteen years old and afraid to face my future.

So I didn't.

At least this is what he *says*.

Fear thuds in my chest. For a minute, I wonder if he's right.

Nah.

I'm dreaming.

The robed ones take colors and put them into my body. Red gives me a jolt, like diving into a cold pool on a hot day. Green is what it feels like when you come out of the water and wrap yourself in a towel: comfortable and warm. Blue makes me sleepy. Sleeping is something I'm good at. I drift off.

It's either a dream or I'm coming down. Except I haven't touched a thing in almost two weeks. Except the beer. I had four cans of Bud before I took the keys to my dad's car. And six more, that I remember, before Tom and I had the race. And that's all that I do remember.

Then...nothing.

The nothing part scares me awake. I struggle to sit up. "Where am I? What's going on?"

Hands hold me down. A wind touches my face. I can't hear what the people around me say. Then I hear a voice I haven't heard in three years. "Keep yer shirt on, Logan. You'll know everything soon enough."

"Gran?" I can't move to turn my head, so Gran appears above me, but she doesn't look sick or wrinkled. She looks way too young to be Gran, except the beady eyes are the same. And so is the large, bumpy nose.

"It's me, Logan. Damn, your timing's bad." Frowning, she puffs on a cigarette. "I've got five hundred on Devil's Pride in the seventh. You could have waited for the race to end before getting antsy."

Gran fades in a buzz of gold light. Someone talks to her. I hear words, but they are all garbled and muffled like someone speaking under water.

If I were dead and in heaven, Gran wouldn't be gambling. She wouldn't be cranky. And she wouldn't still be smoking cigarettes. Or maybe Gran went down instead of up. And I followed her.

Gran is back. Her frown is gone. She smiles. This is a dream all right. The only time Gran smiled was when she won at the track. Gran had been a cranky old bitch. Even before getting lung cancer.

"Excuse me, young man." Her smile slips. "I was *never* a cranky old bitch. And this is no dream, Logan. You're deader than a doornail."

There's more gold buzzing. Gran fades again, but she returns in three blinks. "Let me try that again. Taking your father's car was a stupid move. Not to mention drinking all that beer and trying to impress Hannah by driving like a lunatic. You are dead, Logan. You are not going to wake up in your own bed, late, like you always do. You will never again rush out the door half-dressed. You will never again use your charm to get a good mark, avoid your chores or impress the girls."

Gran turns, speaks to someone I can't see. "He's my grandson. I'll speak to him however I want." She turns back to me. "Face it. You took exit point two. You had written in your life contract that you'd hang on to exit point five. But the next two years of your life were gonna be tough. Tougher than anything you'd go through in the next sixty years. You thought it would be too hard, so you bailed. No surprise there, Logan. You always did take the easy way out."

Seeing Gran makes me feel better. But not in the way you might think. The thing is, I don't believe in life after death. I figure when you're dead, you're history. But Hannah—she's my girlfriend—Hannah thinks that when we die, we're met by the dead people who loved us the most. Remembering this makes me feel way better. Gran loved us, I guess, in her own way. But she loved the horses and herself more. She wouldn't waste her time sitting on heaven's welcoming committee.

"This is a dream, Gran. You don't even look like you."

Gran snorts. "You think I liked looking old?" When I don't answer, she adds, "Being dead has its advantages. I don't need Oil of Olay anymore, plus I can have all the cigarettes I want. And there's a race going on somewhere every day."

Yeah right. "If I was dead, I would have seen that white light everybody talks about." Hannah had told me about that too.

"You cheated yourself by leaving early. In more ways than one," Gran tells me. "Dying by grape would have been less violent. You would have lived long enough to learn what you were supposed to learn. Then when you died, you would have gotten the whole shebang. The tunnel, the light, maybe even an angel or two." She clucks her tongue. "Even I got an angel, Logan. All you got was a massive boom, heat that melted your brain and then nothing."

Gran's words jolt me. I remember. It wasn't quite like that.

It was a boom, a *flash*, melting heat and then nothing.

Until now.

"Holy crap." I start to shake. "Am I *really* dead?"

I might be in heaven but all hell is breaking loose. The tinkling wind-chime sounds grow louder. There's a flurry of movement. Gran fades into the milk-glow sky. "Wait," she cries, "I'm not finished with my grandson yet. There's something else I need to tell him."

But the colors around me get stronger: *zap*, *zap*, *zap*. Hot, cold, sleepy. And the colors take Gran away.

My whole body shakes. My stomach heaves. "What's going on?" My tongue sticks to the roof of my mouth; it's hard to talk. "Where am I?" If I don't sit up… if I don't get something to drink…I'm gonna puke.

Suddenly, there is an extra-large pop in my hand and I am upright. I struggle to adjust my eyes, to figure out where I am.

This place is huge. Open to the sky, to the air. And there are beds. Lots and lots of beds. I peer into the haze. At least I think they're beds. Before I can make sense of things, I see *him* sitting at the end of my bed. The guy who spoke to me earlier.

"Hello, Logan." His eyes—one green, the other blue—study me carefully.

I've never met this guy before.

Yet I know him.

Tattoos crawl up his arms and meet below his neck. "I'm Wade." He pushes frizzy brown hair back from his face, revealing two studs in his left ear.

Wade? To me he's Snakeman. And I've been dreaming of him since I was four years old.

But I've never seen him in 3-D before. And I've never had him reach out and touch me like he does now.

This isn't looking good.

Wade gestures to the pop. "Drink," he says. "Your memorial service is about to start. You're gonna need that to get through it."

Chapter Two

They put something in the pop.

That must be why I feel majorly stoned and blank in the head.

I sort of remember an accident. And being in a hospital talking to Wade. I remember him. But I can't remember what we talked about. Or how I got from that round, white place to where I am now.

Now is a church in Kent, Washington. When I was little, we used to come here at Christmas. I remember that.

I sit beside Wade in the back pew. Organ music plays. Pale October sun shines through the stained glass windows. My school picture is up front, by the altar. It's extra large, like they've blown it up or something. There are flowers all over the place and people too. I might know them, but I might not. It's like my memory is on pause. Only bits and pieces are getting through.

"Why's my picture up there?"

Wade doesn't answer. Feeling stoned, I don't ask a second time. I don't even try to figure it out. It hurts to think. Besides, I don't care. I don't care about anything.

Until I see Mrs. Shields pushing a wheelchair down the aisle.

"That's Tom." Suddenly I am more awake. "My buddy." Tom's legs are in casts. Cuts crisscross his face. Was he in the accident too? I try to remember, but the lead in my head won't go away. "Hey, Tom, what happened? Tom! I'm over here." But he doesn't look at me. He stares at his hands instead. And then his mother wheels him past. "Tom, I'm back here," I call. "Tom!"

"He can't hear you," Wade says.

Wade's full of shit. I open my mouth to argue, but then I see Hannah coming down the aisle between her mother and father. My Hannah. Her long, blond hair is messy straight, not curled and fluffed up like normal. Her face is puffed, her eyes red. She weeps into a tissue.

"Hannah!" I reach out. But she walks too fast. She's gone before I can grab her.

"Everybody's ignoring me!"

"They're not ignoring you," Wade says. "They can't see you."

His words don't make sense. But I don't have time to try and figure them out, because then I see my parents and my sister, Amy. They come out a side door at the front of the church. Dad's bent over like an old man. He's on one side of Mom, Amy's on the other. Mom looks like she can't walk on her own.

I jump up and run down the aisle toward them. Moving sharpens my senses. I recognize people now: Mr. Levesque, my French teacher. The principal, Mrs. Edwards. Casual friends from the swim club. Aunt Susan and Uncle Herb. Plus Tom and Hannah. Brian and Seth. Even their parents. I know everybody here.

Everybody.

My family sits in the front row, just the three of them. "Mom? *Mom*, it's me! Logan." I am so close I can see the purple smudges under her eyes, the wet tips of her eyelashes. Her lower lip trembles. She stares at me, says nothing.

I look at Dad. He whispers in Mom's ear. I smell coffee on his breath. I see a cut on his cheek. I know it's from shaving.

I turn to my sister. "Amy, what's with these two? Talk to me. Tell me what's going on." But Amy's clear gray eyes are shadowed. Her face is pale. She fidgets nervously. Typical nine-year-old. I remember she will be ten soon. Her present is in the car.

Why does the thought of the car leave me shaking?

At the front of the church, a man begins to speak. "We are gathered here today to honor the life of Logan Alexander Freemont." I turn. A minister in white holds a small black book. "Let us pray."

People stand. Voices rise.

So does my panic. It crawls up from my feet and takes over, bit by bit, until the fog in my brain is gone. Until I remember everything.

I am dead.

No way.

I look down. I see my gray sweatshirt. I touch my jeans. The denim is rough under my fingers. I run up and down the aisles, reaching for people. People I know. They slide. Or I slide. Or we both do. Either way, I can't connect.

So I yell. I yell at my parents. At Amy. At Hannah and Tom. "I'm not dead! Look at me, guys, I'm alive. I'm here. It's all a joke. Look!"

The only person who looks at me is Wade. "It's no joke, Logan." He's halfway across the church and his voice is soft and quiet, but I hear him like he's whispering in my ear. "It's real."

"I'm not dead. I'm still me. I still have a body and everything."

"You are still you, but you don't have a body. What you're seeing is a thought form." He points to a tall gold urn up by the minister. "Your body is in there. You were cremated."

Thunk thunk, thunk thunk. My heart pounds in my chest. Dread mushrooms in my stomach. Sweat beads on my forehead. "But everybody knows death is the end. That there's nothing left but matter."

"Death is only the beginning, Logan. Hannah knows that. Lots of people do."

Head rush.

My brain feels like a nuclear explosion waiting to happen. I run to Wade. I grab him by the shoulders, press my fingers into the scaly snakeskin of his tattoos. "If I'm dead, how come I can feel my heart beating? How can I touch you like this? Hear everybody talking? Smell those stupid lilies up there?"

"It's the way it works at first," Wade says. "It'll change when you move on."

"I don't want to move on. I don't want to be dead." What I want is to wake up in my own bed and have all this be a dream.

"It's too late, Logan. You've made your choice."

"I didn't choose. It was an accident."

"There's no such thing as accidents. You chose to die because you didn't want to face your future."

When I was a kid learning to swim, I almost drowned. It's like that now. The same terror, the same helplessness, the same feeling that everything is out of my control.

I hear crying.

And wailing.

It is loud and painful. Frightening.

It is me.

The robed ones come back. They feed me blue. I resist but Wade says, "It'll help."

Soon, a fuzzy calm drops over me. It veils things, like a thin curtain I can see through but not sharply. I hear the service, watch people hug my parents, see them walk down the steps and out of the church, where they kick the leaves and breathe the cold fall air and get on with their lives.

They can go home.

The thought of home takes me there.

We are in the living room and it is filled with people and food. Like a party, only nobody's smiling. My parents sit on the couch. They are surrounded. Grandpop. Amy. Hannah. The talking in the room is like a low rumble. It's there, yet there's something more. Something that scares me.

"I know what people are thinking," I tell Wade. "What they are feeling."

His frizzy brown hair flies out from his face as he nods. "Your awareness is growing."

I don't like it because I have to listen. Mom wonders what she did wrong, how she failed me. Dad feels guilty that we argued, that he insisted I stay with the swimming program. Amy is confused and scared. Grandpop feels like a disappointed old man.

Everyone hurts.

And that's what gets me.

Their pain is so big and so strong that the room cannot keep it in. It seeps out the cracks of the house, down the sidewalk, along the road, into the air. It is a living, breathing thing and it twists my guts in half.

I start to cry. I am too upset to be embarrassed. "I have to let them know that I'm okay."

"You can't do that," Wade says.

"I have to. I need to say goodbye."

"It's not about saying goodbye, Logan. It's about the choices you made. The lives you changed. And where you go from here."

Chapter Three

Wade takes me to a park.

The sky still has that eerie glow. The warm air smells strange, like oranges. And there are flowers all over the place, in colors I have never seen. It's all too weird. But I'm calm. We sit on the grass. There is a weeping willow tree behind us and a big lake in front of us. It reminds me of a place I used to swim in as a kid.

"Is this heaven?" I ask.

"Not exactly. This is more like a way station." Wade gestures to the massive round dome beyond the tree. "That's where they put the colors inside you. To heal your energy field." Then he points across the lake. "But that's where you really want to be."

Where I want to be is home. But I still follow the direction of his finger.

A crystal skyline gleams in the hazy distance. There are other buildings too, huge structures in shapes almost impossible to believe. All reflecting rainbow prisms of light.

"That's heaven?" I ask.

"In a manner of speaking."

Heaven was not all floaty and soft like you might think. It was as real as a full keg on Friday night. Only, so far, not as much fun.

"Who are you?"

"Your guide," Wade says. "I've been with you from the beginning. You have some decisions to make. I'm here to help you."

"I don't want to make decisions. I want to be alive."

"You are alive," he says. "In a different way and in a different place."

I think to myself, This is not the place I want to be.

"You'll get used to it," Wade promises. "Trust me, after a while death will be more real to you than life ever was."

I can't hide a thing from Wade. He knows what I'm thinking.

"Of course I do." He nods. "I know every thought you've ever had. I know everything about you, Logan. What you did in your life, what you should have done, what you didn't do."

Anger bubbles up from somewhere deep inside. "I'm only sixteen. I didn't have enough time to do anything important."

"You'd be surprised at what some people accomplish in sixteen years."

I don't want to hear about other people. I only care about me. And getting back to my family. "If you're my guide," I ask, "why didn't you stop me from getting in that damned car. Why didn't you keep me *alive?*"

"I tried. We discussed that particular temptation at length." He watches me calmly. "You knew your father would push you to stay with the competitive swimming. Your father saw your refusal as another sign of laziness. But it wasn't. You also knew the argument might get out of hand. And you promised me—you promised yourself—that if it did, you would stay and work something out with your dad. Instead, you took your frustrations out behind the wheel of his car. I warned you not to race on Houser Way."

My anger reaches a rolling boil. I am furious at him, furious at myself for being in this unbelievable situation, and I'm scared. I don't want to be dead. "You're lying. You didn't warn me about anything."

"I did. You just don't remember. But you will. In time, you'll remember lots of things." He points to the water. "But for now, watch this."

The water shimmers flat, into a silver screen. Pictures of my life play out in front of me. Not the things I did, but the things I could have done. I see myself graduating from high school; I feel my parents' joy. I see Hannah unexpectedly pregnant; I know there is a problem with our baby. I see Amy surrounded by trouble; I know I am supposed to help her.

"Those were things you wrote into your contract before you were born,"

Wade tells me when the pictures fade. "Things you agreed to do. Now you won't be there to do them. You have altered a mess of probable futures, Logan. Not only have you ended your own life, but you've changed the lives of everyone around you."

I know my parents still hurt. Their pain is inside me, beating where my heart used to be. Suddenly, I am desperate to be alive. I ache with the want of it. I want to go home to Dad's stupid high standards and Mom's "crock-pot surprise" suppers and Amy's constant blabbering. Home to Hannah. "Let me go back! Give me another chance."

"It doesn't work that way."

The accident plays out in slow motion in my mind. I am there again. Laughing with Tom. Waving to Hannah. Getting in the car. Booting the engine. Peeling off in a squeal of rubber. I hear the crash. Feel the heat. Taste blood bubbling in the back of my throat.

It happened. I really am dead. There is no going back. "But I went home for the funeral," I whisper.

"You can hang around the living all you want," Wade says. "All you have to do is think of a person or a place and you are there."

"So I can say goodbye to my folks? Let them know I'm okay?"

Wade hesitates. "You can try, but it takes skill to communicate with the living," he finally says. "And the living have to be willing to see the signs." He shrugs. His snake tattoos ripple up and down his arms. "You can't do much on earth when you're dead. And hanging around doing nothing gets boring fast."

Hanging around doing nothing has always been my number one pick. Now I could do it for the rest of my eternal life.

So why wasn't I smiling?

"You need to move on, Logan. It's harder—you'll have to take the rap for choosing exit point two—but for once you won't be taking the easy way out."

Easy is good. Rap-taking is bad. "Where would I move on to?" I ask warily.

"That depends on how much good you did when you were alive and where you deserve to go."

I feel the fires of hell burning already. I wasn't a bad person. I just wasn't particularly good, if you know what I mean. "I need to let my parents know I'm okay," I say. "I'm going back."

"I don't recommend it," Wade advises. "I'd move on if I were you."

That's when I notice tiny lights— pinprick blobs—off in the distance. They bounce in the air over the lake, and they swirl in groups by the crystal buildings. Instinctively, I know the blobs are people.

Or they were.

The thought is not comforting.

One of the blobs breaks free and floats toward me. The wind picks up. There is a flicker of golden light. The blob grows bigger, more defined. Then Gran stands in front of us, wearing a cherry red dress and a hat the size of a small car.

"Just a minute, Wade. Fill Logan in on the rest of it." She tosses her head, and the purple hat practically topples her over.

"Fill me in on the rest of what?"

But Gran and Wade don't pay attention to me. The two of them stare at each other—a six foot four tattooed Snakeman and a five foot nothing scowling Gran. They are talking without words—I know it—but I can't figure out what they are saying.

Then Gran turns to me. I am struck again by how young she looks. How much thinner she is.

"Just another perk to being dead. You can eat all the Krispy Kremes you want." Gran winks, then turns serious. "Here's how it is, Logan. When you move on, you go across that lake to face the Council. Once you do that, there's no going back. You cut your ties to earth. You cannot be around the living again without permission."

"Then why are you back?" I ask.

"You and I have a history together," Gran says. "And the Council thought it would be easier if you had a familiar face around to help you make your decision."

"Moving on isn't such a bad thing," Wade interrupts. "Seeing the Council is a great honor."

Gran looks at him, rolls her eyes. "A great honor?" She snorts. "You haven't gone before the Council in fifteen hundred years. How would you remember? Those guys are tougher than a general with a prickle in his butt." She turns back to me. "They do your life review. And it's a killer. Every single thought you had, every single thing you did, you go through it all over again. They watch. You watch. If you did good, you feel good. If you did bad, you feel waaaayyy bad. At the end of it all, they want the good to outweigh the bad. They want to know you did the best you could with what you had." Gran quirks her eyebrow at me. "You up for that, Logan?"

It sounds like something Dad put me through on a fairly regular basis. The "you could do more with your life if you tried" lecture. Come to think of it, it sounds like something Gran used to tell me when she was alive too.

I frown. "I don't get it," I say. "Wade says moving on is the better choice. Staying behind is the easy way out. You hate it when I take the easy route."

"Who said anything about taking the easy route?" Gran's hat slides. She reaches up, straightens it. "You want to ace the Council, you go back to earth and do something to make those guys sit up and take notice."

"Arlene," Wade warns, "that's enough."

But Gran pays no attention to him. Her beady brown eyes bore into mine. "You go back and make your life count! You make sure that rat bastard doesn't get to Amy and then you—"

"What rat bastard? What are you talking about?" I ask.

"Arlene, no!" Wade's voice drowns mine out. "You're not supposed to interfere like that."

There is a shuffle of wind, a muffle of words. "He's my grandson. I'll interfere however I like." Then Gran folds in on herself and is gone.

I turn to Wade. "What did she mean? What rat bastard?"

But Wade is silent.

I have no choice now. If there is someone after Amy, I have to go back.

Except, getting there might be tough. There isn't an airport—or even an Amtrak station—in sight.

Chapter Four

I float near the ceiling in Amy's class at school.

The kids are writing. Their heads are bent over their books. It's amazingly quiet for a class of grade fours.

Getting here was amazing too. All I had to do was think "Amy" and then I heard the sucking noise—the same one that took Gran away—and I popped into place. I don't know where Wade is. I don't care.

All I care about is Amy.

And finding whoever Gran was talking about.

Considering the way Gran exaggerates the failings of the male species, I figure the rat bastard is probably some nine-year-old with an attitude. I study the heads of the boys. Which one, I wonder, is bullying Amy?

More to the point, what am I going to do about it?

For a minute, I am surprised and disappointed to find Amy in school. I just died. That ought to be good for at least a week off. But as I look at the orange and brown Thanksgiving decorations on the wall—the turkeys and the horns of plenty—my eyes are drawn to the calendar beside the door.

November 28.

I have been dead a month.

Shock makes me fall from the ceiling. I land in a sprawl on the floor beside Amy's desk. Sitting up, I see the slight pucker of concentration between her eyes and I smell the baby powder scent of her soap.

Love balloons inside my chest. It is like I am seeing my sister for the first time. My love for her is a warm, bursting thing, a strange and unusual thing. I don't think I have ever felt love this big before.

I whisper Amy's name. She does not look up. I raise my voice just a little, automatically glancing at the teacher. Then I remember. No one can hear me.

"Amy," I say in a loud, powerful voice.

Her eyes flicker. She sighs and stops writing. Then she starts up again.

I recall Wade's words: *It takes skill to communicate with the living, and the living have to be willing to see the signs.*

Obviously I lack the skill to send the right sign.

I feel a familiar snap of impatience with myself. Then I hear Wade's voice inside my head.

Relax, he says. *It's not like you have to be anywhere.*

"Yeah, right," I mutter, staring hard at Amy. I wonder who she's scared of. I speak again. "Who's bugging you, Amy? Tell me, okay?"

Slowly, like it is the most natural thing to do, I slide inside Amy's mind. She is writing the words of a story, but she is not concentrating. Her thoughts are a crisscross tangle. She misses me. She is scared she will die too. She is angry. At me for leaving, at Mom for being so sad, at Dad for pretending not to be. A piece of Hannah sits inside her mind too. Hannah has made her feel better about my death. I am grateful for that. Yet underneath everything is the blackness. The fear.

I stare at it, hard. It spills its poison through me in the same way blood flows through arteries.

Amy isn't scared.

Amy is terrified.

And when I see who she is terrified of, I am sickened. I am shocked.

And then I am there beside him.

The cockpit glows with a million buttons, along the walls, in front of me, even on the ceiling. I recognize the airspeed indicator and the altimeter because once, when I was little, he gave me a tour of a plane. Outside the window, I see red lights flashing on the nose tip, wisps of clouds trailing by. It is loud in the cockpit, and warm. But there is a thick, oily *something* hanging in the air that scares me cold.

It is the living, breathing presence of evil.

And it is coming from the rat bastard to my left.

Uncle Herb.

"Throttle back the engine," Uncle Herb tells his co-pilot. "Prepare for landing." He is annoyed. I don't need to see the thin set of his lips to know it. He picks up a handheld radio and speaks into it. "Ladies and gentlemen, Captain Underwood here. Due to heavy fog in Seattle, SeaTac airport is temporarily closed. We are being re-routed to Portland International Airport. On behalf of United Airlines, I apologize for any inconvenience."

I register his words, but mostly I look into his familiar blue eyes. There's a flatness behind them that stretches forever. I shudder. How come I never saw it before?

"Anyone who wishes to deplane in Portland and make other arrangements to get to Seattle," Uncle Herb continues, "please alert a flight attendant. Thank you."

"We're about eight minutes away," the co-pilot tells him when he hangs up the radio.

Uncle Herb nods, busies himself with one of the control panels. "The tower expects us to be grounded overnight," he says. "I was supposed to watch Brad's basketball game. Son of a *bitch*."

The air grows thicker and oilier with his curse. But Uncle Herb isn't thinking of his son at all. He is thinking of Amy. She is going to the game too. He has plans for her.

Plans no adult should ever have for a kid.

For a little girl.

For *my* sister.

His mind slithers and crawls in a million ugly directions.

I don't want to know, but his evil is too strong for me. It sucks me in. I see everything.

Too much.

Uncle Herb as a child. A teenager. An adult. Thinking perverted thoughts. Doing disgusting things. Horrified, I try to pull back, to look away. I can't.

I see him abuse Amy. I watch him cut up her favorite bear, Pookie, and bury it by his hot tub. I feel Amy's terror as Herb says he will do the same to her if she tells.

But what scares me most is that I see the future.

I see how I was supposed to stop him. And how difficult it would be.

I see myself telling. I hear my father yelling, my mother crying. No one can believe—no one *wants* to believe—that Captain Herb Underwood is sexually abusing little girls. That he is sexually abusing Amy.

The family is torn apart. I am responsible.

Suddenly I know this is why I died. This is the future I did not want to face.

Instead I left Amy to face a future without me in it. A future with the rat bastard.

Unless I can figure out a way to stop him.

Chapter Five

"What do you mean, you won't help Amy?"

"Not *won't*, can't. My job is to help you." Wade sits across from me. The eerie glow from the sky has turned his frizzy brown hair into a halo around his head.

We are back in the round, white room. I don't know how I got here, and here is still weird. The sky still vibrates and colors still quiver and ping, but I don't care.

I'm happy to be out of that cockpit.

But I am not happy with what Wade tells me. "You can't let that happen to Amy," I tell him. "She's just a little girl. You have to *do* something!"

My voice disturbs the soothing calm of the round place. The robed ones approach with their colors. Wade sends them away.

"I can't change things," he tells me. "People have free will. Besides, Amy has her own guides. Two, in fact."

Wade sends pictures into my mind.

I see Amy's guides. I know they are there because she is facing a lot in her life. I also know that if I stuck around and lived, I would have earned a second guide. And I would have needed it. Because I would be helping Hannah raise our handicapped son. And I would be revealing Uncle Herb as the rat bastard he really is.

Gran is right. The next two years would have been the hardest of my life.

But I would have faced my fears. I would have grown up. And I would have helped Amy.

Instead I was afraid to try.

Shame burns. I do not look at Wade. Of course it's stupid. He knows what I am thinking. But I do not want to see the disappointment in his eyes.

"It's time to move on, Logan. To accept responsibility for your actions."

Wade wants me to go before the Council, do my life review and cut my ties to the living. But how can I leave Amy?

"There's nothing you can do for her now," Wade tells me.

He is right.

No one would have wanted to believe the truth about Uncle Herb when

I was alive. They're sure not going to believe me now that I'm dead.

Which leaves me dead out of options.

"Oh puuleese!" Gran is back in a burst of gold light. Her energy is so strong that the few robed ones who have been hovering nearby fade into the mist. She wears pink sweats. A cigarette dangles from her mouth. I know she has come from the track. "You can still help Amy. It's just going to be a little harder, that's all."

I don't *do* hard. Even when I swim, I favor the crawl. It's the easiest and most efficient stroke for competing.

Narrowing her eyes, Gran turns to Wade. "I don't suppose you've told Logan the real reason you want him to move on? How you'll benefit from his decision?"

Wade's angelic smile is at odds with the blue and red snakes that crawl up his arms. "No, but I'm sure you'll fill him in."

"When you move on, Wade's job is done," Gran says as she swings back to me. "He retires. No more following you around trying to make you do the right thing."

Gran makes it sound like a life sentence.

"It was," Wade reminds me with a chuckle. Even Gran smirks.

"How can you joke around at a time like this? Amy is in trouble." I feel the oily stink of evil that lurks inside Uncle Herb. The thought of getting close to it again sends a cold shiver down my spine. "Gran, you have to do something! Aunt Susan is your daughter. Go back and tell her what her husband is doing."

"I've been dead too long," Gran says. "Besides, Susan won't listen to me. I didn't like Herb from the moment he set his slimy foot inside our house.

I always told her there was something twisted about him."

She hadn't liked my dad either.

"True enough," Gran admits. "He's too much of a perfectionist."

It is true. And with me gone, Amy will be in for more of Dad's criticisms.

And more of Uncle Herb's attention.

I love my little sister. I love her too much to leave her for the rat bastard. Except evil is more powerful than I ever thought it could be. I don't want to face it again.

"Oh for heaven's sake, Logan, don't be such a weenie." Gran puffs impatiently on her cigarette. "You're more powerful than Herb any day of the week. Go back and haunt the guy, I don't care. Just stop him from hurting Amy."

Wade looks at me. He knows what I am thinking. Either I go forward and face the Council or I go back and face the evil.

Both choices suck.

Especially for someone like me who is used to taking the easy way out.

Suddenly I am struck by a thought. "If this is heaven or something close to it, then that means there's a God."

Wade and Gran nod. For once they agree on something.

"And I assume that God is good?"

They nod a second time.

"Then why would a good God let a bad thing happen to a girl like Amy?"

Gran and Wade exchange glances. Then Gran speaks. "I don't have all the answers, Logan. All I know is that you were supposed to help Amy when you were alive and you messed with the Big Plan. The Council has given me permission to come here and talk some sense into you. If you don't get down there and fix things, Amy's going to pay the price."

I have no choice at all. Amy is what matters.

"You said it takes skill to communicate with the living," I tell Wade, "so show me how to do it."

Love destroys evil.

It will also help me communicate.

Wade has told me this.

I am in my dining room, and dinner is being served. Cutlery clinks against plates. Dad pours water into glasses. We—they—are having store-bought lasagna and bean salad from the deli. I smell tomato sauce, garlic bread. I know the neighbor brought the meal over. Mom has no interest in cooking.

Slipping into my chair, I concentrate on the love I feel for Amy, for my parents, for Hannah. I pull it around me like a cape I wore when I pretended to be Superman as a kid.

I want to be Superman now.

Or at least alive.

Instead I'm a dead guy trying to stop a live guy from hurting my sister.

Mom pushes her food around her plate. Her appetite died with me. She doesn't know how to live now that I'm gone. The only thing keeping her a little bit sane is Amy. "How was school today?" she asks.

Amy shrugs. "Fine." She does not want to talk.

Come on, Amy! I will my sister to open her mouth and tell our parents everything Uncle Herb has done to her in the last eight months. Instead she pushes a piece of pasta around her plate and refuses to say a word.

I want to shake her, yell in her ear, slam my fist on the table and make everyone jump.

But I can't.

Just like I can't materialize in my chair and tell them I'm okay but Herb isn't.

Dead people do materialize. Wade has told me this. But it's rare. Done under special circumstances. And only if a person has earned the right. Earning the right doesn't come down to how much money you've got when you die. It comes down to how much love you gave away when you were alive.

Wade forced me to think hard about that. After a while, I had to face it: The only kind of love I thought of giving away when I was alive involved Hannah and our couch. I haven't earned the right to do much of anything, never mind materialize.

But listen, it's not like the dead are completely useless. We can touch people's minds, go into their dreams, create wind.

No, not that kind of wind. The breeze kind.

I was disappointed until Wade pointed out that dreams can change lives and breezes can grow to be pretty powerful.

I just hoped mine would be powerful enough to stop a rat bastard. And to let my parents know I was okay.

"John, in accounting, gave me tickets to hear the Village Voice choir in Leavenworth next weekend," Dad says before shoving bean salad into his mouth. He is stuffing his feelings, pretending life is normal. "I thought we could go and do a little skiing, maybe wander the village. Herb offered to watch Amy overnight."

Of course he did. The slime bucket.

Mom tenses. She doesn't want to leave the house, my things. Amy's stomach flips. She can't stay there, not again. Dad repeats himself, rattles on about Leavenworth. He is desperate to get away, to forget my death happened.

I concentrate on love and a breeze. The love is supposed to make it easier for the living to see the signs. The breeze is supposed to knock the water jug over, or at least shake the water enough to slosh on the table.

I can't even create a ripple.

"It would be good for us to get away," Dad continues. "Herb says the village is really beautiful at this time of year."

Panic radiates from Amy. She can hardly swallow, she is so scared. I stare at the water jug and try again.

Nothing.

Dad scrapes up the last of his lasagna. "I'll book the hotel."

That's when I see it. A single salt crystal rolling across the table. It stops at the water jug.

It's hardly the breeze I wanted.

And it's hardly enough to stop a rat bastard.

I have my work cut out for me.

Chapter Six

That night, I go into Amy's dream.

Wade has told me how to do it.

I cannot make a dream for her. I have to arrive in one she makes herself. And I must slide in sideways, all natural, like I belong there.

But I also have to make her remember.

I am so desperate to do it right that I am almost afraid to try.

Gran's words mock me. *Don't be a weenie, Logan.*

Gently I touch Amy's mind. She is dreaming a happy dream. I slide inside, sideways, and then wait in the shade of a tree.

Amy rides her bike toward me. Pink streamers fly from her handlebars; her hair blows out behind her like ribbons of taffy candy. I am about to yell "get your helmet," but then I remember it is a dream and it doesn't matter if she has her helmet on or not.

But it's a good way to get her attention, Wade says in my head.

When she gets closer, I call out "Amy!"

She stops, throws her bike to the ground and launches herself into my arms. "Logan!"

I stagger back from the force of her hug. Wade warned me. To the dead, dreams are more real than life. Still, I am surprised at how solid Amy feels.

"I miss you." She squeezes my neck like it's silly putty.

I hug her back. Tears choke the back of my throat. I want to stay with her forever. "You forgot your helmet," I say.

"It's more fun riding without it." She pulls away, studies me with her solemn gray eyes. "Why did you have to die? Where did you go? Mom is so sad. She never stops crying. Dad just pretends you'll be back next week or something."

This is the tricky part. Making my answers big enough that she will remember them in the morning. And tell Mom and Dad. "I'm not dead, Amy. I'm still alive, only I'm somewhere else."

Her face lights up. "So you are coming back?"

"Not really. Not in the way you think."

Her face falls.

"But I am alive and Gran is here and she still goes to the track and you

57

have to tell Mom and Dad that I love them and I'm sorry about taking the car, okay?"

"Okay."

"And Amy?" I hold her chin in the palm of my hand so she can't look away. "You have to tell them about Uncle Herb."

A shadow drops over her face. "I can't."

I tighten my hold. "You have to! He won't hurt you, Amy, not if you tell. I promise he won't. He'll only hurt you if you don't tell. You have to tell Mom and Dad, okay?"

She wiggles out of my grasp and grabs her bike. "I have to go now," she says. "I have to get my rabbit and take it for a walk."

And then she is gone, in a flutter of pink streamers and taffy candy hair.

At breakfast, I whisper into Amy's ear. It takes three tries but she finally says, "I dreamed of Logan last night."

Mom is buttering toast. Her arm stops in mid-air. Dad gulps his coffee. His hand shakes as he puts his cup down. "That's nice."

"He says he's okay and he's still alive."

"Logan is dead, Amy." Dad stands, grabs his suit jacket. "You know that."

"Not in my dream," Amy says stubbornly.

That's the sister I know and love. I keep whispering in her ear.

"He said he is alive and with Gran and she still goes to the track." Amy spoons up the last of her cereal. Her appetite is back. Somewhere deep inside she remembers our hug. It has made her feel better. "He said he is sorry he took the car."

Dad's jaw tightens. He slips on his jacket, kisses Mom on the cheek. "I've got to go." And then he is out the door.

Disappointment rocks me. Amy hasn't said a thing about Herb. I follow her as she gets ready and goes to school—I keep whispering and nudging—but I know she's not going to say anything.

When Amy leaves, Mom goes into my room and sits on my bed. She picks up an old skateboarding T-shirt I wore the day before I died and buries her face in it. Traces of me remain on that shirt. The scent of my deodorant. Feelings from the words I spoke that day, the thoughts I had.

Mom knows it. She sobs. Her body rocks back and forth; her pain fills the room like a heavy, black cloud. I can't stand seeing her like this. I sit beside her, wrap my arms around her. I touch her mind, like Wade showed me, but her grief drowns me. I pull back. This is why I can't go into Mom's dreams. Her grief is too huge. I'm not even sure I can go into her mind.

You can, Wade tells me. *If you do it with love.*

I touch Mom's mind a second time. I think of how much I love her, will always love her. This time, when the warm feeling comes, it is not strange or unusual. It is big and deep and comforting. After a while, Mom feels it too. She stops crying, looks up from my shirt, stares at my school picture on the dresser.

Now is my chance.

I want that picture to fall down. I need Mom to know I am okay.

I have to do better than I did with the water jug.

I focus hard, deep inside myself, as I used to do before the start of a race. I concentrate on wind. On breezes. The air in the room changes. There is a tremor. A slight, faint rocking. Or am I imagining it?

Mom is restless. She stands, thinks maybe it is time she did my last washing.

Or maybe she should go back to work like everyone says. Carefully she folds the T-shirt and lays it back on my bed. She turns to go, brushing past the dresser.

The picture falls.

She stops, turns, stares. Reaches out, picks it up, clutches it to her breast. Her tears start up again.

A part of her believes she knocked the dresser. Another part, the wiser part, knows otherwise.

But Mom does not trust her wise self. Logan is dead, she says silently. Dead and gone.

She puts my picture back on the dresser and leaves the room. How much wind will it take for her to notice I'm right beside her?

Dad is driving a rental car. The Lexus is gone, thanks to me. I know that the insurance company still hasn't settled.

I sit in the passenger seat and watch him weave impatiently through the afternoon rush hour. Horns blare; car lights flash in the waning daylight. He is anxious to get home. His day has been one meeting after another. He is tired.

He is also tired because he has buried his grief. By pushing it aside, he thinks it will not overwhelm him. But it sucks him dry with every breath he takes.

I try to touch Dad's mind; he is too closed. I think about trying the wind thing, but it's too damned hard. Even if I create a bit of a breeze, which is a major long shot, Dad will explain it away.

His cell phone rings. "Robert Freemont here."

"Hey, Freemont, Underwood here."

I hear the conversation as if I were inside Dad's head.

"Hi, Herb, what's up?" Dad says.

"Did you make your hotel reservation for Leavenworth?" Uncle Herb asks.

"Not yet."

"Good, because it's taken care of. A gift from me and Susan. It's the least we can do."

I scream into Dad's ear even though I know he can't hear me. *No, Dad, no! Don't accept.*

He hesitates. "I don't know, Herb, I'll have to talk to Barbara. She's not so keen. Maybe it's too soon."

"It's not. You guys need to get away. The change'll do you good," Herb adds quickly. "Amy too."

At the mention of Amy's name, heat rushes through me. My head feels like it's going to explode. Furious, I holler some more. *Don't go! Blow him off. Don't let him shove you around. He's a scumball!*

A Volkswagen cuts Dad off. He smashes his foot on the brake. Then he says, "Don't push me, Herb. I need time to think about it, okay. I'll get back to you."

He hangs up before Herb can answer.

Jubilant, I do a happy dance in my seat. I need Dad to believe Herb is slime. Trouble is, Dad and Herb go way back. It's not going to be easy.

I talk to Dad all through rush hour. I know he can't hear me, but I tell him everything. And by the time we pull into the driveway, I'm sure I've gotten through. I'm sure he's going to say no to Leavenworth.

I follow him into the house, watch him put his briefcase on the hall table as he has a million times before. Mom is in the kitchen, dishing out dinner. Amy pours water into glasses.

"Susan called," Mom says. "She and Herb booked us into that little hotel in Leavenworth."

Amy's hand slips. Water dribbles onto the table.

"Herb told me," Dad says. "I told him you weren't so sure."

"I've changed my mind." Mom puts a casserole dish on the table. Tuna something. I smell the fish. "It would be good to get away," she says.

Amy smashes the water jug onto the table. Water sloshes everywhere. She runs from the room.

"What's with her?" Dad asks.

Mom shrugs. The two of them stare after my sister.

Me, I stare at the water. Water I failed to spill last night.

And if I had, I know the trip to Leavenworth wouldn't be happening.

Chapter Seven

Angry with myself, I go outside and sit on the front steps. It is a cold, dark night, and overcast. No moon, no stars, no nothing.

I am scared for Amy and I don't know what else to do. Gran's words run through my mind: *Go back and haunt the guy*.

Like I could.

I have no control over anything. Sure, I can think myself anywhere I want to go, but when I get there I can't do anything. And I know for a fact that if Wade wants to pull me back from the world of the living, he can.

Like now.

He tugs on my brain, promising me a couple of cheeseburgers and a double fudge sundae if I'll return to rest and discuss what I've done. I don't need to eat or drink or sleep anymore—it's optional now—but I have a weakness for cheeseburgers and Wade knows it.

Still, I resist.

I want to see Hannah first. She loves Amy. Maybe she can stop Herb.

Hannah's room is on the top floor of her house. She rests in the corner of her pale blue window seat, knees drawn up, hands wrapped around her legs, staring out the window. Top Forty plays softly on her radio. An untouched plate of roast beef and mashed potatoes waits on the floor beside her. I know her family is in the dining room eating dinner. I know Hannah has been excused.

Her eyes are red-rimmed; her skin is blotchy. Hannah has been crying. I stare at her. When did she get to be so beautiful?

I mean, she always was. But now I see her inner light, her glow. Corny? Not to a dead guy. Besides, her glow is so real and so strong that it stretches beyond her body and warms me.

I cannot believe I left her.

I sit opposite her on the window seat.

We were supposed to have a baby together.

Guilt, anger, despair. They rush through me so fast I cannot sort them out. I don't try.

As Hannah gazes out the window, her fingers play with a small medallion at her neck. My St. Christopher medal. I remember giving it to her just before the race.

I'm scared. I don't want to go inside her mind. I'm not scared of what I'll find there; I'm scared I'll never want to leave.

But I have to do it for Amy.

Hannah's mind is open. As soon as I touch it, I see that her sadness is different. She knows I am okay because she believes I am somewhere pure and light-filled. But she is angry I got into my dad's car in the first place. And she feels guilty she didn't stop me.

She knows there was supposed to be more for us.

I impress on her mind that it was my choice, that she shouldn't feel guilty. She pushes the thought away. I send her pictures of the last time we were together—pigging out on pizza and watching *Punch-Drunk Love*. Remembering makes her sadder.

Hopelessness rushes through me. If this isn't hell, I don't know what is.

Wade tugs at me again. He wants me back—to rest, regroup. I tell him no. I need to make Hannah feel better. And I need to tell her about Amy.

Determined, I sweep back into her mind. I flood her with thoughts and feelings and pictures of Amy. Hannah is concerned too. She worries about how Amy is taking my death. I send her pictures of Herb and Amy together, but Hannah's mind won't accept them. Over and over I try until, eventually, I manage to plant a small thought, a tiny seed of worry.

Is it enough?

I don't know.

Then, because I sense Wade growing impatient, I wrap my love around Hannah. I tell her I will always be there for her. Remember our song, I say.

You'll be my Queen; I'll be your King.

Maybe my thoughts do have power, because Van Morrison comes on the radio and he is singing it: "And I'll Be Your Lover Too."

I turn to go. When I look back at Hannah, she is smiling.

"You said it would be tough; you didn't tell me it would be impossible." We are back in the park, Wade and I. The cheeseburgers have not erased my anger. Neither has the hot fudge sundae.

"It's not impossible," he insists, "just difficult. I told you, the living have to be willing to see the signs."

I glare into his blue-and-green-eyed gaze. "And the dead have to be able to make them."

He smiles back. "It takes time to master a new skill, Logan. Don't be so hard on yourself. You're still recovering from your death. Overall, you're doing well. Your presence in Amy's dream was excellent. You touched your mother and father. You even managed to get that song on the radio at just the right time."

"It's not enough." I flop onto the grass and stare into the milk-glow sky. Wade knows the words I have left out: It's not enough to stop a rat bastard.

"This isn't a swim meet," Wade says. "You aren't going to lose if you're two seconds late."

But Amy will lose if I don't keep her away from Herb. And time is running out.

I sit back up. "That reminds me, what's with the time thing? Every time I go back, more time has passed. When I saw Amy at school, they thought I'd been dead a month. I've only been dead a few hours."

When Wade laughs, his frizzy hair bounces and his snake tattoos twist and turn. No wonder this guy gave me nightmares when I was four.

"It's not that funny," I mutter. "What's going on?"

"Time's relative." He grins. "If you'd been paying attention in physics, you'd know that. What takes the blink of an eye over here can take days down there."

Leavenworth is next weekend. Does this mean next weekend is minutes away?

"Relax," Wade says. "Nothing's gonna happen just yet." Another hot fudge sundae appears in front of me. "Eat," he says.

I have to trust him. So I do.

Wanting to hedge my bets, I enter into Hannah's dream that night.

Wade is annoyed with me. He doesn't say so, but I can feel his disapproval. He thinks I need time away from the living.

Hannah is thrilled to see me, but not surprised. She has been waiting. I kiss her and we talk, but when I tell her about Amy and Herb, Hannah does not want to listen.

Hannah is so far from the dark side that she cannot recognize darkness in others. *You have to protect Amy,* I tell her. *You have to tell my parents what's going on.*

But when Hannah wakes up, I am afraid she won't remember our dream.

Next weekend is here.

I don't need to see it to know. I feel Amy's terror, her panic that I am not there to protect her.

At first I do not react. After Hannah's dream, Wade called the robed ones back. They fed me colors and turned me fuzzy calm again. I needed to rest.

But now Amy is in trouble. Her fear is an alarm clock going off in the pit of my stomach.

I am with her in an instant, standing behind her, hands on her shoulders. We are in Susan and Herb's driveway. The sky is blue. The ground shines with frost. It is Saturday, early December. Instead of rain, Seattle is in the middle of an unusual cold snap.

I know all of it. Just like I know the horror that's to come.

My parents wave to us as they pull out. Dad has another brown Lexus. The insurance company settled. I know this too.

Amy trembles; her shoulders shake beneath my hands. I wrap myself around her and hold her close. It is not enough but it is all I can think of to do.

"Let's get this weekend underway!" Herb claps his hands together and smiles his ugly wolf smile. My cousin Brad stands beside him, looking lost in the shadow of his father.

It is the first time I have seen Herb since that time in the cockpit. It is hard to look at him. But when I do, I am relieved. His evil is weaker when there are good people around.

Aunt Susan knows that Amy is unhappy. "We'll run back to your house to pick up that social studies report, Amy. Your mom said you were upset that you forgot it." She wants to make my sister feel better, but she misunderstands the problem.

"We'll do it when Brad's at his soccer game," Herb says to Susan. "I'll drop you and Brad off. Then Amy and I will run over to the house for the homework. We'll probably be back before the warm-up ends."

Susan smiles at my sister. "And we'll go out for pizza after the game, okay?"

Slowly, with great effort, Amy nods.

I want to puke.

Chapter Eight

I did not know ghosts could run.

But then, I'm not a ghost. Because ghosts can appear in front of people.

And if I could do that, I'd appear in front of the rat bastard and scare him to death.

As for the running thing, I'm not doing that either. Whatever I am doing, though, I'm doing it fast.

Because I have to stop this madness.

I go to my parents first. I sit in the car with them, and I yell.

Turn the car around. Go back. Save Amy.

Mom cradles take-out coffee in her hand and looks at Dad. "Maybe we should have brought Amy with us. She was really upset when we drove away."

"She was worried about her social studies report," Dad says. "She'll be fine. Susan said she and Herb have lots of things planned for the weekend."

I shudder and holler some more. *Bad things. Horrible things. Turn the car around.*

"It's only been six weeks since Logan died. Maybe it's too soon to leave her."

Six weeks? How long did Wade make me sleep?

"You heard the counselor," Dad says. "The sooner things return to normal, the better." He flicks on the radio, steps on the gas. He is not going back.

I go to Hannah next. She is in bed, stretching under the covers, thinking of me, thinking of Amy. Amy called her last night. The conversation upset her. Something in Amy's voice wasn't right.

Get up, Hannah. Go to her. Help Amy.

Hannah tosses back her quilt, touches the St. Christopher medal at her neck. She thinks maybe the medal should go to Amy. After a minute, she reconsiders. It is her last physical connection to me. She does not want to give it up.

Hannah disappears into the shower.

The old Logan would have followed her. Or tried to. It's tempting. For maybe a millisecond or two. But I think of Amy and nothing else matters.

What am I going to do? Gran said I could stop Herb. *How, Gran, how?*

I call out to her, but she does not answer. It occurs to me that Gran is disappointed. She knows I am going to fail. I am failing.

I scream for Wade and I hear him inside my head, saying, *Calm down and think*.

How can I think when Amy's fear is choking my mind? When I know they are in the car, they are going to soccer, and soon they will be at our house?

I sit on Hannah's bed and I pray. I do not know what else to do. It is the first time I have prayed since I was a little boy. Even when I died, I didn't. Now I ask God to quit dicking around and to please help Amy. Because Amy deserves to be helped.

When Hannah comes out of the shower, I reach out with my mind and touch hers.

Go to Amy, I say. *Please, be there for her.*

That little seed of worry I planted in Hannah's mind yesterday—weeks ago?—has taken root. She touches the medal around her neck. She decides to go to the house and take Amy for an Egg McMuffin.

I follow Hannah.

As she pulls into our driveway and parks her Volkswagen behind Herb's navy blue SUV, she figures Dad decided to replace the Lexus with something different. Nice color, she thinks as she heads up the sidewalk.

Her knock on the door is unanswered. She frowns. She knows someone is home. She hears the faint stirring of music somewhere in the house.

Kick the damn door open, I yell. *Go find Amy.*

Hannah peers through the glass. Sees Amy's coat on the floor. Two sets of shoes. Impulsively, she reaches for the doorknob and opens the door. "Hello," she calls loudly, stepping into the hall. It is the first time she has been to my house since the service. For a second, she imagines I will walk out of the kitchen half-dressed and smelling of the aftershave she gave me on my birthday. Tears well behind her eyes. She swallows. Her sadness makes me ache. "Anybody home?"

Footsteps sound above her. Amy appears at the top of the stairs. Her blouse is half undone. Her face is marshmallow white. Herb quickly looms behind her. "Oh, Hannah." He is flustered. Red-faced. "Hi."

"Amy?" Hannah stares at my sister. Something isn't right. "What's going on? Where are your mom and dad?"

"They went to Leavenworth for a night." Amy launches herself down the stairs and into Hannah's arms.

"They left me with Auntie Susan and Uncle Herb." My sister is shaking, and she is very, very cold.

"Amy forgot her homework." Herb comes down the stairs behind her. The air grows heavier, oilier. I move closer to Amy and Hannah, stare into the pale blue eyes of the stranger who was my uncle. "When we got here, she complained about a rash on her chest so we were upstairs having a look," he says.

Hannah doesn't recognize the lie. She doesn't even notice Amy's quick little breath when Herb says it. But Hannah notices Herb's pants. Or more specifically, his fly.

It is undone.

Somewhere at the heart of her, Hannah remembers our dream. And she knows there is no rash.

Gently, she tilts Amy's face up. "Are you okay?" she asks softly.

My sister doesn't answer. She looks away, buries her head in Hannah's chest. But not before Hannah sees the truth in Amy's eyes.

"She's fine," Herb bluffs. "I can't see a rash myself, but you know how kids are." He slips on his shoes, grabs Amy's homework from the hall table. "I'll get Susan to have a look when we get back. Come on, Amy. Grab your coat. We have to get to Brad's game."

Don't let him take her, I yell to Hannah. *Keep her safe.*

Hannah's mind clicks over with gear-like precision. She is thinking of what she should do, whether to call my parents, what she will do if she can't find them. She smiles at Herb. "Amy and I had a breakfast date, didn't we, Amy?"

Amy nods. She won't look up.

Herb's eyes narrow. "Barbara and Robert didn't say anything about that."

"They probably forgot," Hannah says breezily. "It's a standing thing, every Saturday since…you know." It is a lie, but she is counting on Herb being made uncomfortable by the unspoken reference to my death. He is. When he doesn't respond, Hannah continues. "We're usually gone about an hour and a half."

Herb wants Amy with him, where he can make sure she stays quiet. "I don't know," he says. "I don't think—"

The pizza flyer interrupts him. I send it scuttling across the floor, flipping and turning on the breeze. Herb watches it land on top of his shoe. Flustered, he wonders, How did that happen? The air is dead calm.

I grin. No it isn't. Not with me around.

"Don't worry about it, Captain Underwood." Hannah uses his title deliberately and then widens her smile as much as she dares. "I'll bring Amy back to your place by noon."

Herb wants to resist, but his blackness is no match for Hannah's goodness. He drops his eyes, bends to pick up the flyer. "By noon," he repeats.

My parents are back by 11:30. They sit in Hannah's living room, perching uneasily on the edge of the sofa. Amy is curled up in Mom's lap. Hannah and her father sit across from them.

"So you didn't actually see anything?" Dad asks Hannah for the third time.

"Amy's shirt was undone," Hannah repeats. "And Herb's fly was down."

When we first stop the rat bastard, I am crazy happy. I follow Amy and Hannah to McDonald's, and I don't even care that I can't eat the food. But now my happiness has dissolved.

"These are serious charges," Mr. Sinclair, Hannah's father, says mildly. He is a lawyer. In spite of that, I like him. I know he believes Hannah. He is just trying to protect her.

"Yes." Hannah nods. "And Amy said Herb touched her and she didn't want to go back to his house."

Mom and Dad exchange glances. Mom is thinking, This can't be happening. Dad is thinking, Hannah has always been melodramatic. My sister is thinking, Now he'll slice me in half like Pookie.

"Amy?" Mom asks softly. "Did Uncle Herb touch you?"

Amy is silent.

Dad tries. "Is there anything you want to tell us, princess?"

Dad! I cry. *Of course she doesn't want to tell you. She doesn't want to believe it happened.*

My sister's voice is muffled in the folds of Mom's sweater. "I don't want to go back there," she says.

As Mom reassures my sister, Dad looks at Hannah and Mr. Sinclair. "I appreciate you calling us. We'll take it from here."

Chapter Nine

He thinks he is going to get away with it.

But he won't. Not if I can help it.

I am in our kitchen with Amy. In the living room, my parents are telling Susan and Herb what Hannah has said.

Amy knows that in a few minutes she will be called out, and she will have to face him. She sits on the edge of the chair, head forward, brown hair curved around her cheeks, staring into her chocolate milk. She wonders how she can make the badness go away. Hannah was supposed to be her friend. Hannah has made things worse.

No she hasn't, Amy.

I blow a breeze across the top of the milk, creating tiny bubbles.

Amy doesn't even smile.

The time for smiles is over.

Amy is still afraid. In fact, she is more afraid than ever. I make her think about truth, and how important it is to be truthful. But Amy believes it is safer to lie.

The air in our kitchen shimmers and flickers. Amy can't see it. I can. My senses are changing, getting sharper. I am more aware of the other side, the side called death. And how it connects with the living.

My body is changing too. When I first died, I looked solid, real. Now when

I look at my hands and legs, I see smudgy shadows. It's like I'm slowly dissolving.

Wade is here somewhere. I feel him. I feel Amy's guides too. They are trying to comfort her and give her the courage to do the right thing.

But my sister...my sister is so young. And this is the hardest thing she has ever gone through.

Witnessing her terror makes me feel as scared and as helpless as I did at my funeral.

I cannot watch.

"You know I would never hurt Amy." The rat bastard leans forward and rests his elbows on his knees. He keeps his wide blue eyes on Mom and Dad. To the living, he is the picture of innocence. Being dead, I see the evil that rides on his shoulders like a spare arm. Like a claw. "I love that kid."

He sits in the green wingback chair; Susan sits in the chair beside him. Mom and Dad are on the couch opposite. Someone has made coffee. Four full cups sit untouched on the coffee table between them.

"Hannah says Amy's shirt was undone." Dad runs a hand through his hair. He is so sick about this, he feels nauseous. "And your fly was too."

Herb's grin is a touch embarrassed. "I'd gone to the john. I was in a hurry to check Amy's rash and get back to Brad's game." He raises an eyebrow. "I don't know why Hannah would be looking down *there*." He pauses just long enough to suggest that Hannah was the one in the wrong. "But if she says my fly was undone, then I guess I forgot to do it up."

You animal, I scream. *You lying bastard.*

There are nods all around. Everyone wants to believe him. They *need* to believe him. If they don't, they will be forced to admit there is a monster in our family.

Mom's voice quavers. "Amy told Hannah you touched her."

"Of course I touched her," Herb says. "I was looking for the rash."

The air in our living room swirls with truth and lies, goodness and evil. Others are here. I sense them crowding around me, watching this horror, yearning for justice.

"I'm sure this is all a misunderstanding." Aunt Susan's eyes flicker nervously. She is yellow with fear.

When they bring Amy into the room, she tucks herself into a tiny spot between Mom and Dad. She will not look at Herb. I think it is a good sign. She is going to rat him out, I tell myself. That's why she won't look at him.

Aunt Susan is the first to speak. "Amy, you know we love you and we would never want to hurt you." Amy nods. "If something is wrong and you don't want to come to our house, we want to know why so we can fix it."

Amy says nothing. She stares at the ground. Pookie can't be fixed, she thinks. And Uncle Herb will fix her too, if she tells.

I don't like where her thoughts are going. I crouch on the floor in front of her. *Tell them, Amy! It's okay. He won't hurt you anymore.*

"Did something happen with Uncle Herb?" Mom asks.

I hold my breath.

Amy nods.

"Did he touch you?" Dad asks.

Amy nods a second time.

Yes!

But then Herb says, "Tell them why, Amy."

Nobody else hears the threat in Herb's voice. But I do. And Amy does too.

It takes her a long time but she finally says, "Because I was itchy and I thought I had a rash." Her voice is so soft, Mom repeats the words.

Dad lets out his breath. "I'm sorry, Herb."

"Hey, it's okay." Herb's lips stretch into a slithery grin. "When it comes to your kids, you can never be too careful."

He is getting away with it.

This can't be happening.

Mom stares at Aunt Susan. Aunt Susan stares back. They are two sisters caught on opposite sides of the same horror. Aunt Susan believes her husband. Mom wants to believe—she needs to believe for Amy's sake—but she isn't sure.

Listen to your instincts, Mom! He's lying.

A tiny frown puckers Mom's forehead. "But if Uncle Herb was just looking at your rash," she asks Amy, "then why don't you want to go to his house anymore?"

There's a hush in the air. Dad and Susan are embarrassed. Herb is angry.

Yes, I think. *Yes!*

Amy doesn't know what to say. So she says the first thing that pops into her mind. "I miss Logan."

The air in the room sags. The other beings retreat, taking their sadness and their disappointment with them. Shocked, I stare at my baby sister.

She had her chance and she blew it.

I can't hold it against her. I blew it too.

"Of course you miss him, honey." Aunt Susan gives her a tender, shaky smile. "We all do."

Ignoring Amy, Herb leans over and squeezes Dad's shoulder. "This has been a hell of a time for you guys," he says softly. "It's no damn wonder Amy is overreacting."

It is over.

I have failed.

Pulling Amy into my arms, I hold her tight. And I cry. It is not enough. It is nothing.

But it is all I can think of to do.

I will not leave her. Wade tugs at me, drags on my energy, pulls on my mind.

Leave me alone, I yell. *I can't leave my sister.*

I won't leave her.

Later that night, when Amy is asleep, my parents come to her room. I sit on the end of her bed and watch while Mom covers her, while Dad checks the catch on her window.

I will be with Amy, I have decided, for the rest of her life. What she goes through, I will go through too. When Herb abuses her again, I will be there. I won't be able to stop it, but I will share Amy's pain.

It is my punishment. I deserve it.

"She hasn't been herself lately," Mom says. They have stopped in Amy's doorway; they watch her sleep.

"None of us have," Dad says. *Because Logan died*, he thinks.

They back away, pull Amy's door shut. Curious, I leave the bedroom and follow them. They settle in the kitchen.

Mom scoops coffee, pours water. Her movements are jerky; her eyes are troubled. "Maybe something did happen but Amy is afraid to tell us." She flicks the switch on the coffeemaker.

Two days ago, I would have jumped up and down, screamed and yelled at her words. I'm finished with that. They can't hear me. And what's the point of trying when I'm going to fail anyway?

"Barbara, we've been over this. Nothing happened," Dad says. "We need to put this behind us."

"Herb's always shown Amy a lot of attention," Mom murmurs. "Too much in a way." The coffee hits the pot with a splatter and a hiss.

Dad's eyes flash angrily. "What are you suggesting?"

Mom shrugs. Her wise self has gotten her attention and it won't let go. "I don't know. Something about this doesn't feel right, that's all."

"This is Herb we're talking about," Dad says. "We've known him for over twenty-five years. He's a father. A husband. A good man."

Mom looks away. "Maybe," she says softly.

Dad glares at her. "Herb is a pilot, for God's sake. A *captain*. Pilots fly planes, keep people safe. They don't go around hurting people."

Mom thinks, *That is the dumbest thing Robert has said in years.*

I agree. Mom knows that evil can wear any uniform.

But I know where Dad is coming from. He won't let himself think that Herb would hurt Amy. If he thought that, he would have to admit that he failed as a father. That he failed to keep his daughter safe.

And for my dad, failure is never an option.

Unlike me. I was born to fail.

Chapter Ten

"Oh, for heaven's sake, Logan, quit feeling sorry for yourself." Gran is beside me. I feel her hand on my arm. I smell cigarette smoke and her musky perfume. "You weren't born to fail any more than I was born to be a supermodel."

We are in a dark, tunnel-like space, whipping up and down hills and going around corners with roller-coaster speed. Brilliant star clusters—or maybe they are entire galaxies—flash by faster than I can blink. I am too stunned to speak. One minute I am in the kitchen with my parents; the next minute I am here. Wherever here is.

Wade's voice comes from my right. "This is the route you took when you died," he says. Back then, you were asleep. Now you're awake."

Up ahead is a warm, welcoming light. I know that beyond it lies the garden, the round building with the robed ones, the crystal city. Wade has yanked me back! "I want to stay with Amy."

"You don't have a choice," Wade says. "You have to come back regularly to recharge."

"You never told me that." The light is growing brighter. We are nearing the end of the tunnel.

"I never told you a lot of things."

We burst out of the tunnel into dazzling brightness. It's like sunlight on steroids. There are others nearby, but I see only vague shapes. I look down at my fading self and realize that pretty soon I'll be a vague shape too. We drift through the warm air. I know without being told that we are heading for the round place.

Gran reaches over and pats my hand. "You did good."

I can't remember Gran ever patting my hand. I wait for her to add, "Too bad you failed." She doesn't. Wade gives me a satisfied nod. I stare from one to the other. "But I didn't stop Herb. Amy's still in trouble. I didn't do good at all."

"Yes, you did. For once, you didn't run away from a challenge," Gran says.

"That wasn't a challenge, that was an *impossibility*." A picture of Amy's scared gray eyes flashes through my mind. And Herb's evil blue ones. Panic rises. "I need to get back. Amy needs me." I try to stop moving, but it's like I'm on a cosmic conveyor belt. A force beyond my control keeps me going forward.

"Keep yer shirt on, Logan," says Gran. "You'll be going back soon enough. You're not done yet."

Wade practically groans. "Arlene, we agreed to give Logan a little time before we told him. He needs to rest."

"Told me what? And what do you mean, I'm not done yet?"

Out of the mist, a slot machine appears. We stop in front of it. "You have to see this!" Gran's brown eyes dance as she pulls me forward.

I don't care about gambling. Not now. Not while Amy's in trouble.

Gran reads my thoughts. "This has nothing to do with gambling and everything to do with your life."

She pulls on the lever. "Remember when Wade asked you to think about the nice things you'd done for people?" Images tumble through each of the three slots, one after another after another.

I remember. Everything I told him, he shot down. He didn't care that I'd done chores or bought people birthday gifts. He was looking for something bigger, like saving somebody's life or volunteering in an African orphanage or something.

"No he wasn't." Gran reads my mind again. "It doesn't have to be a big thing at all. Look." The images slow, then stop. I study the pictures lined up in the three squares. The first one is me, about a year ago. In the second one there's an old woman wearing a tattered parka, struggling with too many grocery bags. In the third one I am there helping her.

"Do you remember?" Wade asks.

I flip back through time, search my mental hard drive, but I can't remember. I shake my head.

"You were walking home last October," Wade says. "She almost dropped a bag of groceries coming out of Albertsons. You went over to help."

Now I remember. The woman was missing a front tooth. And she drove a beat-up old Gremlin. I'd never seen a Gremlin outside of a magazine before.

"That one simple act had a huge impact." Gran pulls the lever a second time. "Watch."

New pictures line up, only this time I get the feelings behind the scenes. I see the woman drive away after I help her put the groceries in her car. She is almost crying. It is the first time anyone has helped her in months. In the second picture she is caught in traffic, but instead of feeling angry and rushed, she is calm. She stops for a pedestrian, then lets two cars merge ahead.

"She's doing those nice things because of you," Gran says. "You touched her inside."

This is too sucky sweet for me. I frown. "No way."

"Yes way," Wade insists. "You did a good deed, Logan. Nobody asked you to do it. Nobody saw you. You did it because it was the right and caring thing to do. Helping that lady was like throwing a stone in a pond. The impact rippled out far beyond what you could see." He points to the last square. "Look."

The image comes alive for me.

The woman is home. She is caring for a man who has cancer. He says something mean to her. I know it's because he is scared, and he is taking out his anger on her. But instead of getting mad back, she soothes him.

She even gets him to laugh a little. I know it is because she feels soothed inside.

I look away. I know the man dies three days later. The woman cries for months. But she will always remember the last time he laughed.

The slot machine fades. We start moving again. For a long time I am too embarrassed to speak. Then I ask, "Why did you show that to me?"

"Because that good deed got you a grace point," Gran says.

I frown. "What's a grace point?"

"An opportunity earned." Wade pushes his frizzy brown hair back from his face; the studs in his ear gleam in the bright light. "Here's how it is. Your Gran went to the Council. She showed them that you were trying to help Amy, that you did a good deed for a stranger. They rewarded you with an opportunity."

"It's not easy getting an audience with those guys," Gran interrupts proudly.

"And they don't give opportunities to any old shmuck either."

"What kind of an opportunity?"

Gran and Wade exchange glances. The last time I was over here, I couldn't pick up their thoughts. This time I can. They are arguing about who gets to tell me.

It's not hard to figure that this opportunity will blow.

"They are giving you the opportunity to materialize in front of one person," Gran says, "in order to save Amy."

"Materialize? You mean, come back to life?"

"Geez, Logan, for a smart kid you can be damned stupid sometimes."

"Arlene!" Wade sighs. "Be nice."

Gran ignores him. "Not materialize as in flesh and blood and bones materialize," she tells me, "but materialize enough that the other person can see you and hear you and know that it's you."

My mind races with possibilities. I could appear in front of Herb and scare the living shit out of him. I could go to Hannah...or to Mom...or to Amy herself.

"But there are conditions." Wade's words snap me back.

"What conditions?"

Wade's blue and green eyes fasten on mine. "You get one shot only. And if the person who sees you doesn't believe, you can't go back and try someone else."

That sucks. Still, I could be there. On earth. *In front of someone.* "Okay."

"There's one other thing." When Gran looks away, I know this isn't going to be good. "If you do materialize," Wade says, "you have to agree to leave the earth plane forever. You have to go across the lake, appear before the Council and get on with your life here. You can't hang around Amy like you've planned."

Leave the earth plane forever? Never see Amy again? Or Mom or Dad or Hannah?

Then something else occurs to me. I begin to sweat. "What if I try and I fail and Herb keeps abusing Amy and I can't go back to protect her?"

This time Gran looks at me. "There's only one solution," she tells me. "You cannot fail."

Chapter Eleven

You cannot fail.

I think about Gran's words all the way back to the round, white place.

They remind me of something Dad repeated before every swim meet: Failure isn't an option.

It was a phrase I came to hate.

"Feed him green," Wade says when the robed ones come close. "Not blue."

He tells them he wants me calm but not sleepy.

The haziness in this huge place has lifted. The lines of my body may be fading, but I see more clearly than I ever have before. I see beyond the beds and the park and the shimmering lake and the crystal city. I see as if I'm standing on a mountaintop looking down.

And I realize something I've never realized before.

I am between two worlds. This is not the best place to be.

Wade sits on one side of my bed. Gran sits on the other. They watch me and wait. They expect me to accept the opportunity they've presented.

I'm not sure I can.

For one thing, I don't want to cross that lake and leave my family forever. For another, how can I pick just one person to materialize in front of? I want to materialize in front of all of them.

"You can't." Wade picks up my last thought. "Besides, there's only one good choice."

"Oh, for heaven's sake, Wade, cut the kid some slack." Gran is irritated. "That's like going to the races and betting on the long shot."

Wade groans and cradles his head in his hands. I know he wants to ream Gran out, but all he says is, "A little encouragement might be in order here, Arlene."

Under different circumstances, I might laugh. Think about it. I'm as close to heaven as I can get without actually walking through the door, and the two people who are supposed to help me are fighting. And here I thought the afterlife was all harps and angels.

Boy, was I wrong.

"We are *not* fighting." Gran's eyes flash. "We are disagreeing is all."

"Who's the person you're disagreeing over?"

Wade starts to speak, but Gran beats him to it. "Your father," she says. "Wade thinks you should materialize in front of him."

My mouth drops open. "Dad?"

"If you materialize in front of anybody else, it'll get right back to your dad," Wade explains. "He'll think they're off their nut. And he won't believe anything they say about Herb."

The thought of performing an "I'm back from the dead" routine on Dad gets my palms sweating. He'd probably kill me. Or he would if I wasn't already dead. "No way." I look to Gran for support.

She won't meet my eyes. "I need a cigarette," she mutters.

"They don't like you smoking in here," Wade says.

She stands. "Guess I'd better leave then."

"No," we both say in unison.

Gran sits back down. "He's right, damn him." She glares at Wade, then turns to me. "If you appear in front of your mom, she won't believe what she's seeing. If you appear before Amy, your parents won't believe her. But if you win your dad over, Amy's got it made in the shade."

I can't do it.

Because it all comes down to *if*.

If I win Dad over. If he believes me. I'm just a dead guy. How am I supposed to convince him about Herb? "No way."

Wade looks at me for a long time. Then he says, "You have an opportunity to change Amy's life. To right a wrong. To undo some of the damage you created by taking exit point two."

And I have another opportunity to fail.

Like I need *that* on my mind for the rest of eternity.

"No." I'd rather play it safe. Even if it does mean living between two worlds forever.

Gran's gaze is reproachful. "You're taking the easy way out again, Logan."

"I'm lazy. I'm supposed to take the easy way out."

"You're not lazy," Wade says softly. "You've never been lazy. But you have taken the easy way out all your life. Do you know why?"

I don't want to answer. I don't even want to think about his question, but I have no choice. This time I don't need a screen on the lake or a slot machine coming out of nowhere. This time, all I need are the pictures in my head and my own guilt.

I've taken the easy way out all my life because I'm afraid to fail. How many sixteen-year-olds do you know who want to admit that?

Like none.

Which is why I've never admitted it before.

But think about it. It's easier to walk away from a challenge than to accept it and risk failing. That's one of the reasons I decided not to go up a level in competitive swimming. I didn't want to spend all that time training, all that time away from Hannah, only to lose by a sixteenth of a second at the finish line.

I'd been down that road so many times, I was sick of it.

But this isn't about swimming, I remind myself. This is about Amy. And this risk is the biggest I've faced in my life.

Or nonlife. Whatever.

If I materialize and stop the rat bastard, I have to leave my family forever. If I materialize but don't stop him, I still have to leave.

Either way, I lose at the finish line.

I don't want to do it. And I don't have to. This is not like some test I have to take in school. I don't have to materialize. I can stay where I am, stay with Amy forever, watch over her.

But I don't need to see the future to know that Herb would continue to abuse Amy. He would *ruin* her. And he would ruin others too.

Dead or not, I can't live with that. I can't leave Amy for Herb. I have to try one last time to stop him. Even if it means leaving everybody I love. And even if I fail in the process.

But appear in front of my old man? No way. "What if I materialize in front of Herb instead?" I ask them. "Give him a heart attack or something?" Now that I'm dead, you probably think I'm supposed to be nice and stuff, but it doesn't work that way. Besides, a heart attack's almost too good for Captain Herb Underwood.

"Herb's gonna live to be eighty-four," Gran says in disgust. "No, it has to be your dad. Besides, he's the perfectionist who made you afraid to take risks in the first place. You might

want to talk about that while you're
down there too."

It is the week before Christmas. I
have been dead seven weeks, two
days, twelve hours and fourteen
minutes.

I have been following Dad around
for three days. When I think the time is
right, Wade will help me take form. I'm
not exactly sure how. He said to leave
the details up to him.

I know tonight is the night. Because
tonight has always been our night. Tree
night. In the past, we would chop the
tree down together, haul it home for
Mom and Amy. It was a guy thing.

Dad did it by himself this year. And
he's thinking about that. He is thinking
about me.

That will make it easier for me to
reach him.

He sits in front of the Christmas tree, drinking his scotch. Everyone else has gone to bed. There are no lights in the living room, but the dying fire brightens things enough that I can see the familiar brown couch, the piano in the corner, the bare tree waiting for tomorrow's decorations.

I stare around the room, once, twice, three times. I want to memorize every detail. Because as soon as I do this, I will leave here and never come back. They say I can come back under special circumstances if the Council lets me. I wouldn't bet my life on it. Even if I had one.

On the mantel is the last family photo taken of the four of us. When I study it, a lump forms in my throat. I see the innocence in Amy's eyes and I know: The picture was taken one month before Herb started abusing her.

I turn and look at Dad. I can't put this off anymore.

I'm ready, I think. Or as ready as I'll ever be.

Send your dad love, Wade replies. *And wait.*

It doesn't feel so weird anymore, the idea of love being a real, physical thing.

The room grows cold. I start to feel heavy. I look down, expecting to see my body take shape. All I see is the same old blur where my arms and legs used to be.

Dad puts his scotch down. He's about to get up, but he looks at the tree and he sees me. I know the exact second it happens. His eyes widen. There's a strangled gasp in the back of his throat. He falls back into his chair.

"My God." He shuts his eyes, rubs them, opens them again. "Hoooolllly shit." He shakes his head just a little. He can't believe what he's seeing.

I speak, even though I know the words won't come out in any kind of sound. Wade says Dad will hear them in his head. "I love you, Dad. Tell Mom and Amy I love them too. And tell them I'm okay. I'm really okay."

Dad is thinking a million things at once. *I've had too much scotch. I am dreaming. I need to wake up. This can't be real.*

And I know I have to make it real; otherwise he won't believe me about Herb. So I grin and say, "Dad, you should have gotten the taller one."

And Dad gets it. I was there with him when he cut the tree down tonight, when he was trying to decide between the tall one or the short one he chose. He knows.

Dad's eyes fill, spill over. His tears run in two straight lines down his cheeks to the edges of his mouth. He knows what he is seeing is real. And he knows, he finally accepts, that I really am dead.

His grief is so huge it's like a kick to my gut. I could drown in it, get swept away. But I can't let that happen because Wade has told me I have to be fast.

"Herb is hurting Amy." I plant a picture in Dad's mind to show him what I mean.

Dad pales, wipes his face, stares at me. His mind flips back to logic. He does not believe what he's seeing. What he's hearing. I try again. "He's doing things to her. You have to stop him."

Dad is unsure. He wavers. Then he rejects the thought. He rejects *me*.

His disbelief makes the room grow warmer. It takes away my power. My heaviness starts to lift. I feel myself growing lighter. Soon I'll fade. I'll never be back. And I haven't helped Amy.

An icy sweat grips me. It cannot end like this. *It can't*. I have to make Dad believe me. I have to give this one last shot. My best shot. For Amy.

Because failure is not an option.

Then it comes to me. I know exactly what to say. How to give Dad the proof he will need.

"Find Pookie! He's buried by Herb's hot tub." I am getting lighter. I rush the words into Dad's head. "Herb cut him up and buried him. To scare Amy." I am fading. Fading. "Ask her."

I am gone.

Chapter Twelve

But I hang around.

Surprising, because I didn't expect to.

I figured I'd be in front of Dad one minute and on that cosmic conveyor belt the next.

Not so.

Don't ask me why. There are still way too many things I don't understand.

Wade is around. I feel him. And the others too. They are becoming more real to me than my own family. I'm not sure how I feel about that. Sad or glad. Maybe a bit of both.

They tell me I have done good. I have done all I can do. They tug on me, urge me to leave, to come to the other side. Not yet, I say. Not yet.

They give me a little more time. Just a little.

Dad does not go to bed. After I fade, he goes into the kitchen and pours himself more scotch. A double. He checks on Amy, on Mom, lets the cat in, out and back in again.

And he paces. I know he is trying to make sense of things, trying to rationalize away what he has seen. What I have told him.

But he can't. Because I am beside him, whispering in his ear. And I believe—I have to believe—that my words, my thoughts, my love for him, have power.

Outside the living-room window, the sky turns. Dawn is coming. Night is fading. I think again of being in a planetarium and watching the sky lighten when the show is over: black to indigo to gray to pearl. And pearl is so close to that milky white of the round place that it reminds me I am running out of time.

Dad puts on the coffee, goes down the hall to shower.

I go to Amy. She is curled up on her side, the covers up to her chin. I brush the hair out of her eyes, smell her baby powder smell, kiss her cheek. She wakes up with a start because she feels something. She feels *me*, only she doesn't know it. Uneasily, she stares around her room. Then she pads down the hall and crawls into bed with Mom.

When Mom pulls her close, I wish I were nine again. That I could do things differently, make better choices, hang on until exit point five.

But I can't.

I drift into my room, sit on the edge of my bed, stare at the pictures on my dresser, the swimming trophies on my shelf, the ball caps I collected. All the details of my life mean so little now. I can hardly relate to them. To the person I was. Maybe because I'm not that person anymore.

In the kitchen, Dad pours coffee, adds sugar, then cream. I hear him slurp. I taste the hot liquid scalding the back of his throat. I smell the tang of his aftershave.

My senses are hyped. I see and hear and feel everything. I hear the cat scratch at her dish, the drip of the faucet in the bathroom, the march of an ant on the sidewalk outside. I feel the steam in the shower stall, the clutch of Dad's fingers around his cup, Mom's arm around Amy.

And even though I am going away, I know I will take a part of this—a part of them—with me.

Dad goes into the bedroom, bends down, kisses Mom's cheek. He whispers in her ear, "I'm going out for an hour. Coffee's made."

I shoot up through my ceiling, out of my roof. I see my yard with the basketball hoop that Dad hung and the garden where Mom grows tomatoes. I see the shed where we store our bikes, our camping gear, our tools.

I float higher. I see Garvin delivering the morning paper, the Christmas lights still on at the Turners' one block over and Hannah's house. She is still sleeping. I feel her breath as though I am breathing myself. I know that she and Tom will end up together. Once that would have angered me. Now I'm glad she'll have someone good in her life.

A slam draws my eyes back to our garden shed. Dad has come out and shut the door. In his hand is a shovel. He goes to his car, opens the trunk, tosses the shovel inside.

He is going to Herb's. He is going for Pookie.

The thought frees me. I relax and drift up. Up.

Below me the streets flow and connect, weaving and linking like the silk of a spider web. Only this web is never-ending.

I see Paine Field and the Space Needle. Lake Washington and Pike Place Market. I see the Cascades, the Snohomish River valley. The Olympic Range and Vancouver Island. Portland, Oregon, and then Utah.

I soar higher, and higher still.

I am dead.

And, yeah, I did die at the wrong time. But it doesn't matter now.

I am going home.